W9-ANQ-490

BUSY BODIES

Play Like the Animals

Copyright © 2011 by David & Zora Aiken
Library of Congress Control Number: 2011927523

All rights reserved. No part of this work may be reproduced or used in any form or by any means—graphic, electronic, or mechanical, including photocopying or information storage and retrieval systems—without written permission from the publisher.
The scanning, uploading and distribution of this book or any part thereof via the Internet or via any other means without the permission of the publisher is illegal and punishable by law. Please purchase only authorized editions and do not participate in or encourage the electronic piracy of copyrighted materials.
"Schiffer," "Schiffer Publishing Ltd. & Design," and the "Design of pen and inkwell" are registered trademarks of Schiffer Publishing Ltd.
Type set in Kids BT

ISBN: 978-0-7643-3832-8
Printed in China

Schiffer Books are available at special discounts for bulk purchases for sales promotions or premiums. Special editions, including personalized covers, corporate imprints, and excerpts can be created in large quantities for special needs. For more information contact the publisher:

Published by Schiffer Publishing Ltd.
4880 Lower Valley Road
Atglen, PA 19310
Phone: (610) 593-1777; Fax: (610) 593-2002
E-mail: Info@schifferbooks.com

For the largest selection of fine reference books on this and related subjects, please visit our website at **www.schifferbooks.com**
We are always looking for people to write books on new and related subjects. If you have an idea for a book please contact us at the above address.

This book may be purchased from the publisher. Include $5.00 for shipping. Please try your bookstore first. You may write for a free catalog.
In Europe, Schiffer books are distributed by
Bushwood Books
6 Marksbury Ave.
Kew Gardens
Surrey TW9 4JF England
Phone: 44 (0) 20 8392 8585; Fax: 44 (0) 20 8392 9876
E-mail: info@bushwoodbooks.co.uk
Website: www.bushwoodbooks.co.uk

BUSY BODIES

Play Like the Animals

David & Zora Aiken

Illustration by David Aiken

for Tenley
Zora Aiken

David Aiken

Who leaps like a frog
Or hops like a bunny?
You can if you try.
It's fun and it's funny.

Get down on all fours,
Sneak out of the house.
If you hear, *"mee-ooow!"*
You'll SCURRY like a mouse!

Scrunch down on the ground,
And think, "itty bitty."
Be slow and be quiet,
And CREEP like a kitty.

Prance 'round in circles,
And head for the course.
Then when the bell sounds,
Just GALLOP like a horse.

Bend elbows and wrists,
And hold your hands funny.
Stoop down to get set,
Then HOP like a bunny.

First listen for danger.
Is anything near?
If you should sense trouble,
RUN fast like a deer.

Pretend you're in water.
(Don't jump in for real!)
Lie flat on your tummy,
And SLIDE like a seal.

Now hold your head high.
Not low like a seagull.
Then stretch out your arms,
And FLAP like an eagle.

Just squat down in place,
Hands flat on a log.
Then jump through the air,
To LEAP like a frog.

Curl into a ball,
As tight as you dare.
Roll over and over,
To TUMBLE like a bear.

Stand straight on all fours.
Look back—that's a rule.
Now watch for your chance,
To KICK like a mule!

Hold arms up and out,
And wish yourself luck.
Now stick out your fanny,
And WADDLE like a duck.

You don't have a tail
To swing from a tree.
But find the right rope,
And CLIMB like a monkey.

How high can you jump?
See what you can do.
Pretend you're on springs,
And JUMP like a 'roo!

(That's kangaroo!)

You've played lots of critters,
But don't think you're through.
To see what you've missed,
Go look in the zoo!